DETECTIVE DINOSAUR
UNDERCOVER

by James Skofield
pictures by R. W. Alley

HARPER

An Imprint of HarperCollinsPublishers

For Bill and Dutchie; for
Lori and David
—J.S.

To the dinosaur lovers
at Sowams, Nayatt, and
Primrose Hill
—R.W.A.

HarperCollins® and I Can Read Book® are trademarks of HarperCollins Publishers.

Library of Congress Cataloging-in-Publication Data
Skofield, James.
    Detective Dinosaur undercover / by James Skofield ; pictures by R.W. Alley. — 1st ed.
       p.   cm. — (An I can read book)
    Summary: In three brief mysteries, Detective Dinosaur learns about doing undercover work, gets chased by strange blobs, and finds rain on a sunny day.
    ISBN 978-0-06-623878-4 (trade bdg.)
    [1. Mystery and detective stories.   2. Dinosaurs—Fiction.]   I. Alley, R. W. (Robert W.), ill. II. Title.
PZ7.S62835Dk   2010   2008055605
[E]—dc22   CIP
                                                                         AC

10 11 12 13 14   SCP   10 9 8 7 6 5 4 3 2 1

❖

First Edition

Contents

Dinosaurs in the story

Tyrannosaurus	(tih-ran-uh-SAW-russ)
Pterodactyl	(ter-eh-DAK-tul)
Diplodocus	(dip-LAH-duh-cuss)

Brrriing!

The telephone rang

in Detective Dinosaur's office.

It was Chief Tyrannosaurus.

"Come to my office,

Detective Dinosaur," said the Chief.

"I have some undercover work for you."

"Okay, Chief,"

said Detective Dinosaur.

"I will be right over!"

He laced up his shoes.

Detective Dinosaur

pinned on his badge.

He pulled on his vest.

"Something is missing,"

he said to himself.

"I know!" said Detective Dinosaur.

"The Chief said

this was undercover work.

I had better cover up."

Detective Dinosaur

put on his overcoat.

He pulled on his gloves.

He plopped his hat on his head

and slipped on his dark glasses.

"Hmmm," said Detective Dinosaur,

"I'm still not completely undercover."

Detective Dinosaur

stuffed the sofa cushions

into his overcoat.

He draped a blanket

over his shoulders.

He clipped papers all over himself.

"Oh, dear!" said Detective Dinosaur.

"Undercover work is tiring!"

Detective Dinosaur

emptied his wastebasket onto the floor.

He placed it over his head.

It was very dark.

"There!" said Detective Dinosaur.

"Now I am truly undercover!"

Detective Dinosaur left his office.

He could not see.

He bumped over

to Chief Tyrannosaurus's office.

The Chief was surprised.

"Who are you?" he growled.

"It's me, Detective Dinosaur,"

said Detective Dinosaur,

"reporting for undercover duty."

Chief Tyrannosaurus laughed.

"Oh, Detective Dinosaur," he said,

"undercover means 'in disguise.'

Take off that silly outfit!"

Detective Dinosaur

took the wastebasket off his head.

He shed the blanket,

took the cushions out of his overcoat,

removed his dark glasses,

hat, gloves, and overcoat,

and sat down.

"There," said Chief Tyrannosaurus,

"now I can see you!"

Detective Dinosaur said,

"Yes, Chief," and yawned.

"I think undercover work

is too tiring for me.

I need a nap!"

Case Two

Under Covers

Detective Dinosaur took a nap

in his office.

He had a dream.

In his dream,

Detective Dinosaur was being chased

by two large, scary blobs.

Each time he looked,

the blobs were right behind him.

When he stopped running,

the blobs stopped.

When he started running again,

the blobs started running, too.

"Oh, drat!"

said Detective Dinosaur in his dream.

"This is very alarming!

I can't get away

from these awful blobs!

Go away!" he shouted at the blobs.

Detective Dinosaur shouted so loudly

he woke himself up.

"Thank goodness it was only a dream!"

said Detective Dinosaur.

He began to sit up.

As he sat up,

he noticed two large blobs

moving toward him under the blanket.

Detective Dinosaur froze.

The blobs froze, too.

Very slowly, Detective Dinosaur

began to lie back down,

and the blobs backed away from him.

"It was not just a dream,"

said Detective Dinosaur.

"It is happening to me right now!

Help! Help! Help!" he shouted.

From all over the police station,

officers came running.

Officer Pterodactyl,

Deputy Diplodocus,

Cadet Kitty,

and Chief Tyrannosaurus

all crowded into the office.

"What is the matter?"

asked Chief Tyrannosaurus.

"Oh, Chief," said Detective Dinosaur,

"I had a bad dream.

I was being chased by blobs!

When I woke up,

I found it was true.

Watch!"

Detective Dinosaur began to sit up,

and the blobs moved under his blanket.

Just then Cadet Kitty

pounced on the moving blobs.

"Brave Kitty!"

yelled Detective Dinosaur.

"Ouch! Get those blobs!

Ouch! OUCH!"

Officer Pterodactyl giggled.

"Those are not blobs," she said.

"Those are your feet!"

She pulled back the blanket,

and there were

Detective Dinosaur's feet.

Everyone left

Detective Dinosaur's office.

Cadet Kitty curled up on the blanket
and closed her eyes.

Detective Dinosaur patted her.

"Brave Kitty," he said softly,

"if those blobs come back,

you arrest them!"

CASE
CLOSED

Case Three

Under the Weather

It was a bright, sunny day.

Detective Dinosaur

and Officer Pterodactyl

were on patrol.

They stopped to buy some fruit

at Ricky Raptor's Fruit Market.

Officer Pterodactyl chose

a big, green apple.

Detective Dinosaur chose

a round, yellow pear.

Officer Pterodactyl went to pay.

Detective Dinosaur

was about to step outside

when he noticed it was raining.

Detective Dinosaur went over
to Officer Pterodactyl.
"We must eat our fruit inside,"
he said.
"It has started to rain."

"You must be imagining things, sir,"

said Officer Pterodactyl.

"It is a bright, sunny day!

Look!"

Detective Dinosaur turned around.

Dinosaurs were strolling past

in the warm sunshine.

"Go on outside, sir,"

said Officer Pterodactyl.

"I will join you when I have paid."

37

Detective Dinosaur

stepped onto the sidewalk.

SPLOOOOSH!

A spray of cold water

hit Detective Dinosaur on the head.

He ducked back under the awning.

"That is very wet sunshine,"

said Detective Dinosaur to himself.

Officer Pterodactyl joined him.

"Why, sir," she said,

"you are all wet!"

"I told you it was raining,"

said Detective Dinosaur.

"How mysterious,"

said Officer Pterodactyl.

"It looks sunny to me."

"So you say,"

sputtered Detective Dinosaur.

"You try stepping outside."

Officer Pterodactyl stepped out

onto the sidewalk.

The warm sun shone down on her.

"There, you see?"

asked Officer Pterodactyl.

"Now come on out!"

Slowly Detective Dinosaur

stepped out from under the awning.

SPLAAAAAAAAASH!

A flood of cold water

hit him in the face.

"Oh! I am sorry!"

said a voice.

Detective Dinosaur

and Officer Pterodactyl looked up.

Rowena Raptor held a watering can.

"I was watering my flowers,"

called Rowena,

"but I did not mean to water you!"

"Next time be more careful, ma'am,"

said Officer Pterodactyl.

Detective Dinosaur went back

inside the fruit stand.

"May I borrow an umbrella?"

he asked Ricky Raptor.

"Certainly, Detective Dinosaur,"

said Ricky Raptor.

He brought out a big plaid umbrella.

"Thank you," said Detective Dinosaur.

He stepped back outside.

"There!" he said.

"Now I am ready for anything!"

"But, sir," said Officer Pterodactyl,

"it really is a beautiful day!"

"You never know,"

said Detective Dinosaur.

"The weather around here

can change so quickly!"

Together, the two friends
walked on down the street
and ate their fruit
in the warm sunshine.